For Ringo, who let us all be Texans ✦ *Sarah Burell*

For Nikki, my wife and best friend ✦ *Bryan Langdo*

———————— ★ ————————

STERLING and the distinctive Sterling logo are registered trademarks of
Sterling Publishing Co., Inc.

Library of Congress Cataloging-in-Publication Data
Burell, Sarah.
Diamond Jim Dandy and the sheriff / by Sarah Burell ; illustrated by Bryan Langdo.
p. cm.
Summary: When a friendly and talented rattlesnake slithers into Dustpan, Texas, he must prove his value to
the residents of the town before the sheriff will allow him to stay.
ISBN 978-1-4027-5737-2
[1. Rattlesnakes--Fiction. 2. Snakes--Fiction. 3. Babies--Fiction. 4. West (U.S.)--Fiction.] I. Langdo, Bryan,
ill. II. Title.
PZ7.B91625Di 2009
[E]--dc22

2008013767
Lot#: 11/09
2 4 6 8 10 9 7 5 3 1

Published by Sterling Publishing Co., Inc.
387 Park Avenue South, New York, NY 10016
Text © 2010 by Sarah Burell
Illustrations © 2010 by Bryan Langdo
Distributed in Canada by Sterling Publishing
c/o Canadian Manda Group, 165 Dufferin Street
Toronto, Ontario, Canada M6K 3H6
Distributed in the United Kingdom by GMC Distribution Services
Castle Place, 166 High Street, Lewes, East Sussex, England BN7 1XU
Distributed in Australia by Capricorn Link (Australia) Pty. Ltd.
P.O. Box 704, Windsor, NSW 2756, Australia

Printed in China
All rights reserved

Sterling ISBN 978-1-4027-5737-2

For information about custom editions, special sales, premium and
corporate purchases, please contact Sterling Special Sales
Department at 800-805-5489 or specialsales@sterlingpublishing.com.

Book design by Mina Chung

DIAMOND JIM DANDY

and the SHERIFF

by **Sarah Burell**

illustrated by **Bryan Langdo**

STERLING

New York / London

Nothing exciting ever happened in Dustpan, Texas.

The menfolk snoozed at Earl's Feed Store.

The ladies dozed at their sewing circle.

The kids drifted off in school and drooled all over their books.
The town sheriff took up babysitting just to pass the time.

One day, the sheriff was rocking Idie Mae Tumbleweed
when a rattlesnake slithered into town.

"Holey Buckets!"
he cried.

The rattlesnake smiled at the sheriff, like he was trying to make a friend. He smiled so big, his pearly white fangs sparkled in the sunshine.

"I can see you're a neighborly sort of snake," said the sheriff, "but folks around here don't like rattlers. I'm afraid you're not welcome here, pardner."

The snake looked terribly disappointed. He slithered away,
his rattles dragging across the dusty ground.

The sheriff was putting Idie Mae in her playpen when he heard a loud commotion at Earl's.

"**Dang!**" he cried. "Something's actually happening in Dustpan!" He hoisted Idie Mae to his hip and rushed to the feed store.

The menfolk were clapping and cheering. The rattlesnake was balanced on a bale of hay, performing for the customers. He tied himself into one fancy knot after another.

"Best show I've seen," said One-Eyed Bill. "That snake's got talent!"

The sheriff was fit to be tied. "You can bet your boots the ladies won't like a snake," he said.

Suddenly, Idie Mae cried out for her bottle.

"Don't move, pardner," he said to the snake. "I'll be right back."

The sheriff took off.

So did the snake.

On his way back to Earl's Feed Store, the sheriff heard a chorus of oooh's and aaah's coming from the Town Meeting Hall. Inside, he found the Dustpan Ladies' Sewing Circle. The rattlesnake was posing and the ladies were admiring the diamond pattern on his back.

"**Look!**" said Odette Hicks. "I embroidered a diamond on my bloomers!" Odette's bloomers reminded the sheriff he had to change Idie Mae's diaper. This time he left in a hurry.

So did the snake.

The sheriff was walking back to the meeting hall to have a little talk with the snake when he heard squeals of laughter coming from the schoolhouse. The snake zigzagged back and forth across the schoolyard. Twenty-seven kids zigzagged back and forth behind him.

"Dadgum it," said the sheriff. "Even the kids like the snake."

The sheriff called a town meeting at the courthouse. He set Idie Mae
on the steps and paced back and forth.

"Irritatin' rattler,"
he fumed.

The townsfolk arrived and the rattlesnake came, too. The sheriff spoke loud and clear. "Citizens of Dustpan," he said. "I'm runnin' that rattler out of town."

"But he's entertaining," cried the menfolk.
"He's inspiring," said the ladies.
"He's our friend," shouted the kids.

"It's the Law of the West!" shouted the sheriff. "Folks aren't supposed to like rattlers—even friendly ones." He snapped his suspenders and escorted the rattlesnake to the edge of town.

Before the snake slithered away, he looked back and smiled at his new friends. It was the saddest smile ever seen in Dustpan, Texas.

All of a sudden, everyone heard a loud shriek.
"**Where's Idie Mae?**" cried Mrs. Tumbleweed.

The sheriff had been so hopped up over the rattlesnake,
he'd forgotten all about her.

"Where could she be?" cried the sheriff.

Everyone had a different idea.

"Maybe she's crawled to Vernalee's Hair Salon," said Odette.

"Idie Mae doesn't have much hair," said Earl. "She's probably crawled to Lucky's Bar-B-Q."

"She can't eat barbeque," said Odette. "She only has two teeth."

"Maybe she's crawled to Deadman's Gulch," said One-Eyed Bill.

Mrs. Tumbleweed fainted.

The sheriff wiped a tear from his eye.

The citizens of Dustpan gathered at the rim of Deadman's Gulch.

No one wanted to look over the edge.

"Listen," whispered One-Eyed Bill.

"I hear rattling," said Odette.

EVERYONE heard **rattling!**

The rattlesnake was coiled up on a ledge, rattling his tail for Idie Mae, who was giggling and cooing and clapping her hands.

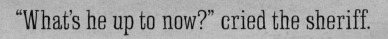

"What's he up to now?" cried the sheriff.

Just then, Idie Mae grabbed the snake's rattles.
Everyone gasped.

Idie Mae was falling into Deadman's Gulch and she was pulling the snake down with her!

The snake wedged his pearly white fangs into
a crevice in the rocks. Then, with every bit of
strength he had, he pulled Idie Mae

up,

up,

up out of Deadman's Gulch . . .

...and tossed her right smack dab into her mother's waiting arms.

"I've never seen anything like it!" said Earl.

"He's a hero," gushed Odette.

Even the sheriff was convinced. "That is one jim-dandy snake," he said.

The citizens of Dustpan named the snake Diamond Jim Dandy.

The sheriff made him his deputy.

And everyone was pleased as punch to have a rattlesnake in town.

Especially the babies.

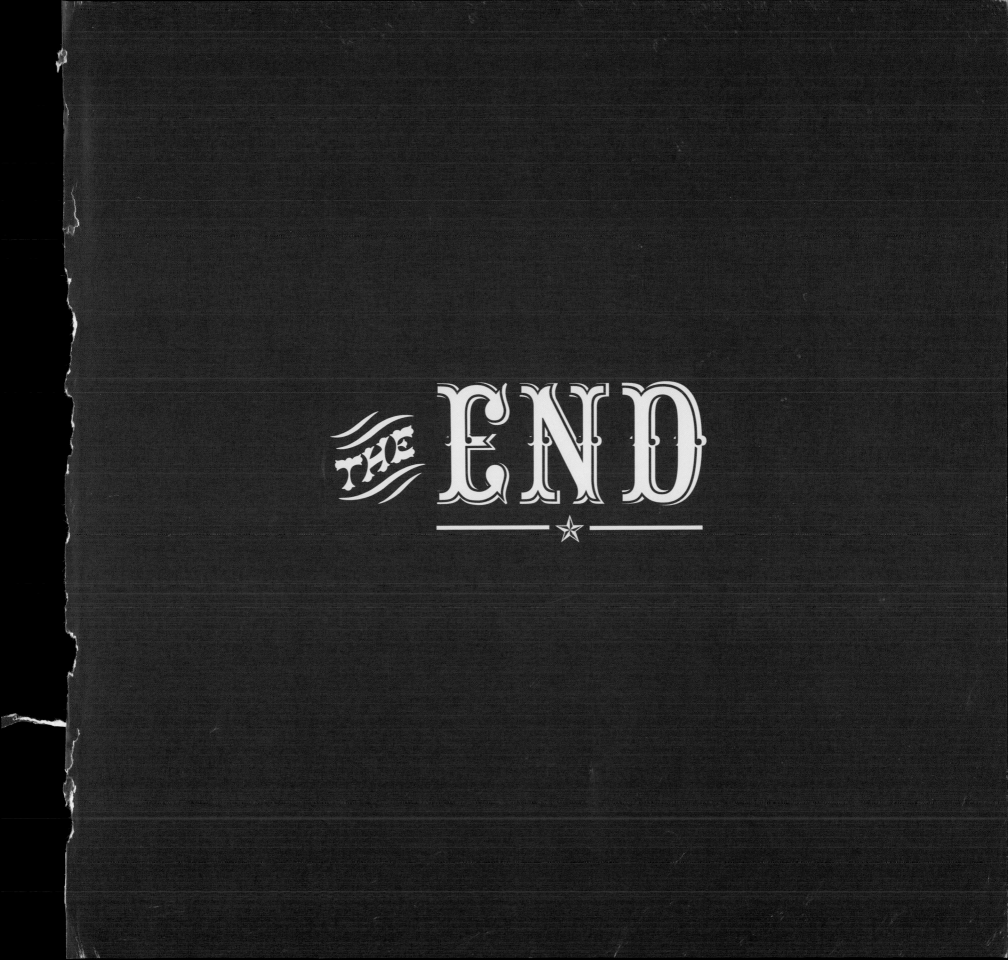